THE AFTERGLOW OF WAR

LESSONS LEARNED

PHIL EMMERT

First edition 2015
Published in the USA by *thewordverve inc.* (**www.thewordverve.com**)

eBook ISBN: 978-1-941251-36-2
Paperback ISBN: 978-1-941251-37-9

Library of Congress Control Number: 2015934686

The Afterglow of War: Lessons Learned
A Book with Verve by thewordverve inc.

Cover and interior design by Robin Krauss
www.bookformatters.com

eBook formatting by Bob Houston
facebook.com/eBookFormatting

DEDICATION

I dedicate this book to my wife, Beatrice "Bea" Emmert, for her encouragement and inspiration in both my writing and in my ministry.

A wife of noble character who can find? She is worth far more than rubies.

Proverbs 31:10

FOREWORD

The writer of Ecclesiastes said it well.

To everything there is a season, and a time to every purpose under the heaven.

There is indeed.

A time to love, and a time to hate; a time of war, and a time of peace.

(Ecclesiastes 3:8)

Peace finally came to our town. This book is about that peaceful time, which began in 1945.

TABLE OF CONTENTS

CHAPTER 1

PEACE AT LAST

Looking up into the clear, blue Indiana sky, my best friend Peanut and I heard it, but could not find it. The "it" was a sound like we had never heard before. It was a cross between a roar, a growl, and a whine. It was not an animal nor was it human. It had to be some sort of machine or aircraft because it was coming from above the clouds. We never saw it that evening.

A couple of days later, we heard it again. Only this time it was louder and closer. Suddenly, like a silver streak, it flashed in the sky, just for an instant. It was indeed some sort of aircraft. We only caught a glimpse of it. Was it a craft from outer space? What was it the paper called these things? UFOs—unidentified flying objects. Well, it certainly was that to Peanut and me. We only got a fleeting look at it, but it was the sound that made the hair stand up on the back of my neck. Peanut looked at me, and his eyes were as big as doorknobs.

"What in the Sam Hill was that?" we blurted out in

unison. The local paper told us what it was in print that evening.

Through the years since, I have heard this sound many times, and always get a thrill. The *Booneville Reporter* said it was a jet plane that the people in our small town had seen and heard. Jet. I liked the sound of the word: Jet. Jet. Yes, I loved to say it.

A few days later at the Avon Theater uptown, we got a good look at one of these planes. A newsreel showed what America had come up with just before the end of the war. However, it had never flown in battle. It was still kind of experimental, but the Army, Air Force, and Navy wanted to order a bunch of them. These aircrafts were said to fly over five hundred miles per hour. And they were powered by Allison jet engines that were manufactured over in Indianapolis, just twenty-five miles from Booneville.

We could not imagine anything going five hundred miles an hour. We had never ridden more than thirty-five miles per hour. That was the speed limit during the war years. Of course, you could drive as fast as you wanted now that the speed limit had been lifted. But we didn't have a car, so I still didn't know the thrill of speed.

It was October 1946, and the leaves on the trees were ablaze with color. It was a wonderful time to be a boy in a small Midwestern town. The horrible war had been over for a year. That rascal, Hitler, rather than face a war crimes trial, had committed suicide when he saw Germany was defeated. We had gotten revenge for the sneak attack on Pearl Harbor by completely wiping out two Japanese cities, Hiroshima and Nagasaki, with a single bomb on each city. These two bombs had finally brought unconditional surrender and ended the war.

Everyday living was slowly returning to normal. Food, gas, and tires were no longer rationed, but some things were still very hard to find. Coffee, sugar, and bananas were among the things that were still scarce. Momma could now buy nylon hose again and had at least five pairs on hand.

A rumor was floating around, that Winklers factory would soon stop making mortar shells altogether and would go back to making coal stokers. The workforce had already been cut back to one shift. Momma, having been laid off, had been home with us kids for the last ten months. We hoped Daddy would not be laid off.

Our servicemen had been slowly coming home as their enlistments were up. Consequently, jobs were starting to become hard to find. My own uncles and cousin came home this last spring. Two of my uncles came back and were given their former jobs at Winklers Factory. Another uncle came back and began to farm. My wounded Marine cousin bought a truck and began to haul lime and fertilizer for a living. But doctors at the veteran's hospital picked shrapnel out of him for years.

The upside was, with men coming home and getting

married, more and larger houses would be needed. Families were already starting to grow, so the building trade would likely pick up. We never saw so many ladies who looked like they had swallowed watermelons. It was called a "baby boom" and led to the "housing boom." This of course added other manufacturing jobs. In a couple of years, anyone who wanted a job had one.

The car factories that had retooled to make jeeps, trucks, tanks, and airplanes in 1942 had just started to make cars again. The first full model year would be 1947. From the pictures of the new models we had seen, the factories must have still been using the 1941 blueprints. With the exception of one particular car, they sure looked a lot like the 1941 models. Gasoline was no longer scarce. More and more cars were seen on the road as people got their cars off the blocks and out of barns and sheds where they had been stored during the war.

Jerry Mount, our neighbor across the alley, had recently arrived home from serving in the Navy. He said he had just ordered a brand new Studebaker automobile. They were made right there in Indiana, up in South Bend. Jerry showed Peanut and me a picture of it out of a shiny advertisement booklet. It was a strange-looking car. One could hardly tell the front from the back. I jokingly asked him, "How will you know if you are coming or going?"

He just laughed and said, "All cars will look like this someday, Willie." He always called me Willie.

Thanksgiving and Christmas were really nice that year. Food was plentiful. Stores were alive with people shopping. Everyone seemed a little more cheerful and full of the holiday spirit. For Christmas, I got a set of silver Roy Rogers pistols with a gun belt and holsters. They came complete with a box of caps so that when you shot them, they sounded somewhat like a shot, or more like a very small firecracker. Pop, pop, pop. And you could smell the gunpowder as the smoke came out of the barrel.

All the neighborhood kids, as well as Peanut and I, no longer played Army. We now played cowboys, Indians, and Old West bank robbers. We also played a lot of baseball and basketball. I guess we played basketball almost every day.

In the winter, our hands would get so cold, we lost the feeling in our fingers. However, basketball was the major sport in the Hoosier State. All the neighborhood boys pretended we were on the winning team in the state basketball tourney. We all wanted to make the winning last-second shot.

In the summer, we played baseball in our backyard. The old baseball got ragged and lost the cover, so we wrapped tape around it to hold it together. We only had one old, broken bat, and we repaired that with tape too.

Home plate was the cement slab at the old lean-to of a back porch. When the door was closed, that was our backstop. First base was the telephone pole by the alley, second base was the green apple tree, and third base was one post on the grape arbor. It was a lopsided diamond, but it worked for us. If you hit the ball through the open window in the coal shed, it was a home run. If you fouled the ball four times, you were out. We usually only had four or five kids on a team. And no girls were allowed to play.

One day just after my birthday in June, Peanut came running into the kitchen where I was nursing a Coke by pouring it into a small glass. I was pretending it was whisky and that I was sitting at a poker table in an old Western saloon. If my folks had seen me doing this, they would have given me a beating. Our family was what was known as "teetotalers."

Well anyway, Peanut was so excited he was stuttering.

"Slow down, man," I said. "What in the world is wrong?"

He started over and said, "Do you want to take a Red Cross lifesaving course?"

I said, "Where, when, and what does it cost?" Because if it cost anything, I knew that was out.

He said, "It's free and it starts next week at the swimming pool. Every morning you go and they give these free lessons. It's great; you get to go in the water for free every morning."

So that afternoon we went to the pool in the Booneville Park and signed up. We had to take a paper home for our folks to sign, but that would be no problem.

The next week, we began our lifesaving course. The first thing they wanted to do was to teach us how to swim. Well, sir, I had been swimming almost as long as I could walk and roller-skate. But I played along and did it just like they told us. After a few days of this, we began the lifesaving part where you had to save someone who was drowning.

Peanut and I both had a problem. Neither of us was big and muscular. I weighed maybe seventy pounds soaking wet, and Peanut was smaller than I was. We liked to say we were "wiry," which was a polite word for scrawny. I did okay saving Peanut and any girl that was about my size.

Then they ran a ringer in on me. It was a big ole teenage boy who pretended like he was scared and fought me off. Actually, he almost drowned me. But all's well that ends well. At the end of the month, we were all given a certificate of completion. However, all that summer I secretly hoped no one would need me to save them. Thankfully, there were paid lifeguards for that.

THE HEART ATTACK

Early in 1945 before the war ended, my daddy tried to enlist in the Army. America was getting down to drafting older men with children. Daddy wanted to serve on his own terms, so he went to enlist. When he went for his physical, the Army doctor asked him how long he had had his heart condition. Daddy never, ever went to a doctor, and so he told the doctor that he didn't have a heart condition. The doctor said, "Yes, you do, and you need to see your family doctor about it." Well, you guessed it. He didn't go.

Less than two years later, Daddy had a heart attack that put him in bed for some time. Our lives changed drastically after this. In the 1940s, a heart attack was either fatal or it would completely disable you. There was no such thing as heart surgery or even medications for the heart. Morphine was the major treatment for the pain. And it was addictive.

Needless to say, Daddy couldn't work. And so Momma

went to work as a clerk at Haag Drug Store. Momma wore many hats. She was a wife, Momma, cook, bread earner, nurse, and disciplinarian.

I only wore one hat. I was a child, as was my older sister Mary Anne. Mary Anne and I didn't make it any easier for Momma. We often squabbled with each other. As the older sister, she thought she was my boss. And I knew she wasn't my boss or my Momma.

Momma expected us to do chores around the house. I saw no need to do chores, because you just had to do them again the next day. Why make the bed when you were going to get back in it? Why not wait until there were no clean dishes before washing a dish? Sweep the floors? They would just need to be swept the next day. This was my philosophy: Don't do today what you can put off until tomorrow. What if tomorrow never came? Wasted work.

Before my daddy got sick, if he had to speak more than once to us kids, he would whip us with his belt. Momma, on the other hand, made us go cut a switch to use on us. A switch hurt me more than a belt, especially in the summer when I wore short pants.

One day I had not done my chores, and when Momma came home, she told me to go cut a switch. I became really smart-mouthed and sassed her. My bad! When I saw her outside cutting her own switch, I ran around the house to

my beloved cherry tree. I climbed up in it as far as I could go. Momma came out with her switch and glared at me. When she said, "You had better get down here right now," I shook my head and stared back.

"William Henry, I am giving you to the count of ten to be on the ground!" She had fire in her eyes. I didn't see her mad very often, but this was one of those times.

Well, sir, I knew my Momma could climb a tree as good as I could. And I also knew when she got to me, she would throw me out of that tree! By the time she got to five, I was on the ground in front of her, ready to take my stripes, which I knew I had coming. *Lesson learned.*

Mary Anne and I always bickered over who would wash and who would dry the dishes. Our old house only had cold, running water. We had to heat water on the cook stove. After heating the water and pouring it in a wash pan, we would wash, rinse, and dry the dishes. We were squabbling, fussing, and getting more water on the floor than on the dishes. We finally got them done about the time Momma walked in the door from work. She saw all the water on the floor and made us mop the kitchen. The job had to pass inspection before we left the kitchen that night. *Lesson learned.*

CHAPTER 3

SOFT SUMMER NIGHTS

Our town was much different from modern towns of the same size. I never remember a violent crime being committed while I was growing up. Crime consisted of window peepers and petty theft.

There was a man named Ralph in our town who was noted for looking in the ladies' windows at night. Ralph showed up more than once at our house. One night he was looking in our window and really scared Mary Anne. She screamed, and he ran.

Momma, Daddy, and the elderly neighbor man talked the situation over and came up with a plan. Momma started keeping hot water simmering on the stove. One summer night the window was open and the shades were up in Daddy and Momma's bedroom. Daddy was bedfast at this time. Momma got a glimpse of Ralph at the bedroom window. She didn't let on that she had seen him. She sat on the bed, held Daddy's hand, and talked softly to him. She asked Daddy—loud enough for someone outside the window to hear—if he would like a cup of coffee. Then Momma went to the kitchen and dipped out a nice, steaming, hot cup of water from the stove. Coming back into the room, she purposely opened her robe a little to expose some flesh and pretended she was taking coffee to Daddy. When she got even with the window, there was Ralph, with his eyes wide open. He had become really interested now. Well, sir, Momma let it fly right in Ralph's face. He must have howled for a block as he fled. I don't believe old Ralph ever peeped in our windows again. *Lesson learned.* Maybe you can teach an old dog new tricks.

Sometimes on summer evenings, the neighborhood kids would play hide and seek or kick the can. One night just after dark, we were playing one of these games that required tagging someone before they reached base. I was running full tilt around our house. I forgot one little detail—the low-hanging clothesline in our backyard. Someone had taken the prop out from under it, and the clothesline was just about chin high to me. It caught me under the chin and threw me up in the air and backward about four feet. Then gravity took over, and I hit the ground on my back. I was choking and had the breath knocked out of me, all at the same time. Thinking back, it is a wonder we survived childhood in those days. *Lesson learned.* Don't run in the dark.

CHAPTER 4

OLD BUCK

He was black and white with a black saddle across his back. He stood knee-high to my Momma and weighed about forty pounds. Buck was his name, and he was the best friend I ever had for about thirteen years. Buck was a Border Collie mix. He had no sheep to herd, so he kept watch over me and my family.

He didn't know a lot of tricks, but I could dress him up and put him in any position and he would stay that way. When I felt mistreated, Buck was always there to kiss me on the cheek, and all he asked for was a pat on the head, a scratch on the belly, and a cookie now and then.

We acquired Buck as a pup in 1941. By 1954, he had become blind and deaf, and he was easily confused after we moved from the only home he had ever known. Sadly, one day he wandered onto the busy highway in front of our house. Rest in peace, dear, old, loyal Buck.

And so our summers were occupied with chores,

roller-skating on the sidewalks, baseball, basketball, swimming, and kick-the-can. I often recapture and relive in my mind those innocent summers between 1946 and 1954. But times were changing.

CHAPTER 5

NOT UP TO THE JOB

Sometime in 1947, several of the older boys were talking about making good money caddying for the local golfers at the Green Links Country Club. All you had to do was carry a golf bag and hand clubs to the man you were caddying for. Well, it sounded like an easy way to make some money to me.

Now I didn't have the first clue about golf. My daddy said it was a rich man's game. He said only bankers, lawyers, and other crooks played golf. To me it kind of looked like a fancy way of wasting time. Whack the ball, walk a couple of hundred yards, and whack it again.

When I got to the country club for what I learned later would be eighteen holes of golf, I was looking to carry somebody's bag. There was an older man dressed in knickerbockers and long, loud socks, who didn't seem to have a caddy. I walked up and timidly asked if he needed a caddy. He asked my name, where I lived, and who my daddy was. As he looked me over, he turned up his nose, like something smelled bad. I knew it wasn't me; I had taken a shower after swimming yesterday.

Finally, he seemed satisfied and motioned toward his golf bag. I picked up the bag with a grunt. From a distance, it didn't look that heavy. But believe me, it was. I slung the strap over my shoulder and followed the man wherever he went. I learned quickly. Don't talk when someone is addressing the ball. That's fancy talk for getting ready to whack it.

I also learned some flowery language that day that my folks never used. Most of that language was calling the ball or the club something. I cannot repeat these words in this account. By about the fifth hole, I was slam worn out and had a whole new vocabulary. Sometime later, I would try out some of those words.

The fellows who were playing kept talking about a birdie, but I never saw one. Par was good but under par was better. And one of the fellows was handicapped, but I think he was faking it because he looked all right to me. They had me stomping little bits of sod, called divots, back in place. I was supposed to hand the man a wood or an iron. I had no idea which one of the clubs was a wood or what in the world a five iron was. The only iron I had ever seen was the one Momma used on our clothes on washday.

I barely made it through nine holes. The foursome was standing around the clubhouse drinking beer, and I was waiting to be paid. About that time, one of them said something about playing the back nine. I about fainted and said, "I don't feel good; I need to go home." The man I was toting for looked a little disgusted. But he peeled off five dollars from a roll of bills and told me to get on home. He didn't have to say it again. I took the money and slinked toward home.

That five dollars made me feel a lot better. I was glad to go back to collecting and selling soda bottles for two cents a bottle. Now, that was my first and last experience with golf until I was above forty years old. However, this was another *lesson learned.* There are certain jobs a person cannot do.

CHAPTER 6

TROUBLE FOR DADDY

I mentioned that our family was not drinkers. We never had beer, liquor, or wine in the house. Momma and Daddy just did not believe in drinking. However, as previously mentioned, there was no good treatment for heart conditions in those days.

Dr. Ballard, our family doctor, had his own theory about stimulating the heart. He told Momma that she should give Daddy a teaspoonful of whisky once every day to stimulate his heart.

Daddy about exploded, but Momma convinced him that it was only like taking medicine. To Daddy, it was . . . because he couldn't stand the taste of it. In those days, the drugstore sold whisky and wine. Momma discreetly brought a pint of "Four Roses" whisky home and put it behind the block of ice in the icebox. Every day when she got off work, she would retrieve the whisky from behind the block of ice and make Daddy take his "medicine." He would almost gag and made a horrible face when he took it.

Mary Anne and I thought it was funny. Kids will be kids. One day Mary Anne said, "William, what do you think whisky tastes like?"

I shrugged my shoulders and said, "Shucks, Sis, I don't know."

Then she said, "Do you want to taste it to see?"

Since I was always the timid one, I said, "No, Momma would skin us."

Mary Anne came back with, "Silly, she doesn't have to know!"

I had a feeling this probably was not going to end well, but not only was I timid, I was weak. Mary Anne needed a partner in this crime. She was able to talk me into imbibing along with her. I guess it is true most people don't like to drink alone.

Mary Anne got two small glasses off the drainboard on the sink, went to the icebox, and got out the bottle of Four Roses. She poured a little in both glasses, just a smidgen. She said, "Go ahead."

Getting a little bolder, I said, "Let's make a toast." We had seen way too many movies. We clicked our glasses and I took as big a swallow as I dared, and lost my breath! I thought my throat was on fire! Seriously. After I got my breath back, I said, "You know, in the movies they put some water or coke with it."

So we split a warm coke and poured it on the remaining swallow of Four Roses in our glasses.

We finally got down what she had poured, but my head felt funny. The room looked funny. Everything suddenly seemed funny to me. I even laughed at Mary Anne. But we quickly came back to reality. We needed to cover our tracks. We each washed our glasses and put everything back like it was. We were home free—almost.

Momma was a pretty sharp lady. Unbeknownst to us was the fact that Momma was keeping a sharp eye on the whisky. When she got home from work, she went to give Daddy his "medicine." As she poured out the spoonful into a glass, she eyeballed the bottle. She became suspicious, flew into Daddy's room, and said, "Robert O. Henry, have you been in the whisky?" She sounded more like his Momma than his wife. And it was more of a statement than a question.

Daddy didn't know what to say but you could tell he was hurt and shocked. Momma didn't realize it, but she almost caused both Daddy and me to have a heart attack. Daddy finally said, "Annie, you know I don't like the taste of that stuff. No, I didn't drink any!"

Mary Anne was lurking outside the doorway. Momma whirled around and quickly asked her if she knew anything about it. Now let me tell you something about Mary Anne Henry. She could lie like a rug on a floor. There was no way you could tell if she was lying. "Why, no, Momma, I sure don't know anything about it, and I'm sure William doesn't," she said in wide-eyed innocence.

Now when Momma had begun to question Mary Anne, I went out the back door and down to Peanut's house. You see, I could never lie worth anything, especially to my Momma.

Thankfully, Momma and Daddy were in a big discussion by this time, and I was never asked about the incident. However, from that day forward, Momma marked the bottle after she gave Daddy his dose of medicine. I really don't think she believed Daddy. And yet, another *lesson learned*.

CHAPTER 7

THE PIE INCIDENT

Sometime in the late 1940s, one of the bread companies began to bring boxed pies to Dillon's Store. One September afternoon, Momma called me in the house and said she wanted to surprise Daddy with a nice dessert for supper. She told me to go to the store and buy a chocolate pie if they had one, because chocolate was one of Daddy's favorites.

Back from the store, I said, "Here's the pie, Momma," as I carefully placed it on the table. Momma took the pie and put it up in the cupboard. I am not absolutely sure of the rest of the menu but pretty sure it was fried ham, fried potatoes, gravy, and string beans.

We washed up and sat down to eat. When the meat and taters had been eaten, Momma went to the cupboard and got the pie out. She cut one piece and before she sat it on the table, she said, "This just doesn't look right."

We all looked at it, smelled it, and finally, Daddy said, "I'll give it a try." He brought a forkful of chocolate pie to his mouth. But it didn't stay in his mouth. He spit it out and said, "Dang, that tastes horrible." We all gave it a small taste test—and it was indeed horrible.

Momma said, "You kids take this pie back to the store and tell Ed it's spoiled." So Mary Anne picked up the pie, and I tagged along, hoping when Ed gave us our money back I could buy a Hershey bar and a Coke. We walked to the store down the back alley.

All of a sudden, Mary Anne said, "Think fast!" and tossed the pie my way. Well, I didn't think fast enough, and it landed upside down. I picked the boxed pie up and, just as quickly, tossed it to her.

"Back at you," I retorted.

Mary Anne never was very athletic. She missed, and it landed right side up at her feet. We fussed with each other and tossed the pie some more. When we arrived at Dillon's Store, I made sure the box was closed up really good. Mary Anne marched in, held out the pie box, and announced, "Ed, this pie is not good," in her most grown-up, bossy voice.

Ed Dillon was a very nice man about fifty years of age. He was one of those people who never showed much emotion over anything. Ed took the boxed pie and opened it. He looked down, and for just an instant, I thought I saw a smile. Then he said, "It sure doesn't look very good, does it?" He didn't say anything else. We lived in a time when the customer was always right.

He went to the big, old, silver and black cash register, punched a button, and cranked the handle. The sign in the little window of the cash register read NO SALE. He reached in, got the fifty cents, and handed it to Mary Anne. I was about to ask for a candy bar, but Mary Anne was already out the door.

I am pretty sure Ed probably asked Momma about the pie next time she was there. But fortunately, the bad pie incident was never mentioned again.

CHAPTER 8

EXPERIMENTING WITH A NEW LANGUAGE

Let me set the background for this account. I had several cousins and when we got together, we usually got into trouble. One particular cousin and I got into trouble together on more than one occasion. Dave was a little younger than I was, but far more adventuresome.

We had an old-maid aunt who owned a farm. She was my daddy's aunt and my great-aunt. Aunt Lola would take us in her old "Model A" out to her farm, and we would pump water for her cattle and hogs. For boys living a sedate life in town, it was a wonderful adventure. It didn't seem like work to us to hand-pump gallons and gallons of water.

One of my daddy's brothers and his wife lived in the house on the farm. They were straight-laced Christian people who went to church twice on Sunday and once in the middle of the week.

Now don't get me wrong; we sure were never a perfect family by any means. We got angry and spoke harshly to each other at times. But as previously mentioned, Momma and Daddy never cussed. Nor did our extended family ever use coarse language. But kids like to experiment with new things. Dave and I were no exception.

Dave and I were almost a quarter of a mile from the house where the hogs were enclosed in a large pasture. We were supposed to pump water and throw some ear corn out for the hogs. I recalled some of the language I had heard on the golf course on the one day I tried to caddy.

I bragged to Dave that I knew some pretty salty language. He, of course, wanted to know what it was. So I told him a few of the words I had learned. He came back with, "Shucks, I know those words." I didn't believe him.

So I started saying some of them. And he started saying the ones he knew. And we got louder and louder. As we called out these dirty words, they kind of echoed off the old barn. We really liked the sound of it, and pretty soon we were shouting them as loud as we could.

In about five minutes, Mikey, Dave's little brother, came running up all out of breath. He had been playing in the yard at the house. He caught his breath and blurted out, "You guys better shut up; they can hear you up at the house! They couldn't understand exactly what you were hollering, but I thought it sounded like bad words!"

Well, sir, we shut up but were now afraid and ashamed

to go to the house. What if they understood any of the words we were saying? We just knew we would get beat half to death.

We finally had to go to the house because it was getting late and we were getting hungry. We just hoped when we got there we wouldn't have to eat a bar of soap. We put on our most innocent looks and went up to the house. My Uncle John asked, "What were you guys doing down there at the barn?"

"Oh, nothing," Dave spoke up. "We were just calling the hogs." Dave was almost as good a liar as my sister. We got away with it that time. But we tucked this experience away with a mental note to never again use that language where adults could hear. *Lesson learned.*

CHAPTER 9

THE RODEO

Some people think life on the farm is boring. But kids have a way of spicing it up. My Aunt Lola rented the tillable ground out to another farmer. But she kept at least twenty acres to run hogs and cattle on. We kids loved to pump water and feed the animals. When my cousin Dave and I went out to the farm with Aunt Lola, together we invented new adventures.

Dave had a great imagination. One day Dave said, "Let's have a rodeo." I looked at him like he had lost his mind. He said, "No really, let's have a bull riding contest, just like in a rodeo."

Well, we had no bulls except for the two bull calves that were not even half-grown. One was a Guernsey and the other was a Holstein. Now, not far from the house was a large barn. The barn had four small box stalls with a manger in each one. The cows, calves, and hogs all ran together in the lot around the barn.

We would need a little help with this rodeo. Dave

convinced his little brother Mikey to help us. The plan was to fasten the calves up in the box stalls and then ride them out the door and stay on as long as we could. The one who stayed on the longest would be the champion.

Coaxing the calves into the barn with a bucket of ground oats and corn was easy. We found a small section of picket fence with which to pen the calf up against the manger so we could mount it. Mikey would open the outside door when we told him.

Dave had a nickel in his pocket, and so we decided we would flip to see who went first. Dave won. *He thought.* I took the section of picket fence and forced the calf over against the manger. Now let me say that neither of these calves was very wild because we fed, watered, and petted them quite often.

There was not much of a struggle as I pushed the Holstein over against the manger. This was to change drastically in a short time. I told Mikey as soon as I took the picket fencing away, he was to open the outside door.

Dave was on the manger, and the calf was wedged against it. Dave put one leg over our "Brahma bull" and dropped down on him. He held him as tightly as possible with his arms and legs. I took the fence away, and Mikey opened the door. Well, sir, when that calf passed me, his eyes were big as saucers. Dave was laughing and shouting.

That calf saw daylight and was out the door in one

giant leap. I ran to the door in time to see that calf jump in the air again and make a sharp left turn at the same time. One thousand one, one thousand two, one thousand three—that is as far as I got.

It looked like there were about two feet of space between Dave and the calf. Dave went up in the air, and the calf ran out from under him. When Dave came down, he landed on his backside in a fresh pile of cow manure. We call these piles "cow patties." I laughed so hard the tears ran down my face.

As Dave got up, the expression on his face was priceless. And for once in his life, he was speechless. Then I congratulated him. "You win, Champ!"

I was not about to get on the other calf. I don't think Dave ever forgave me for not taking my turn. We swore Mikey to silence, and to make sure, Dave bribed him with the nickel he had in his pocket. Dave washed himself and his pants off in the watering tank. And once again, a *lesson learned.*

CHAPTER 10

A SAD DAY

It seems that in childhood we are often on an emotional roller coaster. We are either exuberant or we are very sad. I remember a few sad days as a child growing up. But one of the worst was the day Peanut moved away. We had been inseparable for almost six years. In the summer of 1948, Peanut's mother got a good job as a secretary in Indianapolis at the Allison Aircraft Engine Factory. Since she was divorced and was the only breadwinner in the family, she took the job.

As the movers were loading the big Mayflower moving van, Peanut and I exchanged a couple of gifts to remember each other by. I gave him an old yo-yo that needed to have a new string on it and two pretty rocks I had found in Prairie Creek. He gave me his ridiculous-looking, homemade "Tommy Gun" that had seen us through many a battle back during the war. As dumb as it looked, I was glad to get it. Something to remind me of him every time I looked at it.

Late in the afternoon in the middle of July, that van was all loaded, along with his mother's old Plymouth. We promised we would keep in touch. But that was the last time we ever saw each other. Nor did we ever write or call each other. Peanut petted old Buck one last time. There must have been some pollen in the air. Peanut's eyes were all red, and mine were stinging something fierce. I have a snapshot in my mind of Peanut staring out the back glass of that old Plymouth. I quickly turned my back, listened for the car to turn the corner . . . and then he was gone.

I often think of Peanut. Is he still alive? What does he look like after all these years? Does he have children and grandchildren? Does he ever think of me? From time to time, I think about trying to locate him. Then I realize I never knew his full name or his mother's name. After all these years, it would be impossible to locate him. Besides, what would we talk about now?

Another *lesson learned*. Keep your promises. Hang on to good friends as long as you can. Don't let them just slip away.

CHAPTER 11

TIME TO MOVE ON

It seems Dr. Ballard's treatment worked on Daddy. As you recall, it was a teaspoonful of Four Roses whisky once a day, bed rest, and a shot of morphine . . . which he finally had to wean Daddy from.

Daddy gradually built up his strength. The summer months were especially kind to him. He sat in his rocker on the front porch and also took short walks. Then he began to walk around the block. He seldom got in the bed during the day. In 1950, Doctor Ballard said country living would be better for Daddy. There was a lot of soot in the air in the winter. Most people still heated with coal and the rest with oil. Both systems kept the air saturated with heavy, black smoke.

Momma still worked at the drugstore. Daddy found a house on the highway about six miles from town. It was an old farmhouse that was in better shape than the house in town. Uncle Donald moved all our furniture in his farm truck, with the help of Uncle Johnny and my cousin Tommy.

This house sat back from the road and was right on a Greyhound bus route. They ran a local that Momma could take to within a block of the drugstore. Daddy got stronger after this move. Life was not any easier for us as we had to pump water by hand. However, it was in the kitchen. There was no inside toilet, but it was a short walk to the outhouse. We didn't mind that so much except when it was really cold or if the wind was coming from the wrong direction in the summer. We kept a pot in the house so we didn't have to make the trip at night. I drew the short straw and had to take that pot to the outhouse every morning.

Daddy felt and looked so much better, so he went to the highway department for a job. Now Daddy was a Democrat, and they were in control of the state at that time. He pulled some strings and got a job driving a state highway truck. It was a pretty good job in those days. He hauled rock and asphalt. He always had someone riding with him. They drove the roads looking for road kill and making sure potholes were filled.

Daddy never had to get out of the truck unless he wanted to. He just drove, and his helper did the hard stuff. Winter was a little tough on him. He once worked plowing snow for thirty-six hours straight. He stopped by the house once or twice for sandwiches and coffee. He did let his helper plow snow while he caught a catnap on the passenger side.

Now that both Momma and Daddy were working, they decided they needed a car so that they didn't have to depend on the bus. Now Daddy's credit was not all that good because of his illness. So he found a used car dealer who let him buy an old car "on time." He could pay the man every payday, and within six months or so, it was paid for.

Now let me say right off that these cars were not cream puffs. The first car Daddy brought home was a 1937 Plymouth that could lay down a smoke screen the military would have been proud of. When we went to the gas station, we always put in a quart of oil and checked the gas gauge. It used almost as much oil as it did gas.

I want to tell you about the tires we used. Daddy did not believe in new tires. He bought used tires. I called them "used-up" tires. We put what was called "boots" in the tires so the inner tube would not be punctured by pebbles on the road. When we rode along, the tires went bumpity-bump, bumpity-bump. We were constantly airing them up and changing tires. Daddy and I got so good at changing tires I think we could have been in a pit crew at the Indianapolis 500.

When that old car would run no more, we traded it for a 1939 Plymouth. It didn't smoke, but if the temperature was below thirty degrees, we had to push it off to start it. Fortunately, the driveway was downhill to the road and we could start it by getting it rolling, pulling out the choke, and popping the clutch. I remember this car well. It was the first car I ever drove . . . when the folks were gone.

I said to myself one day, "William, you have watched Momma and Daddy drive this thing. You will never learn any younger." I retrieved the key off the nail in the kitchen and got in the car. I was in luck. It was a fairly warm day. I started it up just like I had seen Momma and Daddy do it. I ground it into gear, which was the wrong gear, and it bucked and then died. Finally, I got it in the right gear and drove it to the end of the drive at the road. No place to turn around down there, so I finally found reverse. Third time was the charm.

I backed that baby up the drive to where it had been parked. Now that I had all the gears figured out, I did this again. It became kind of boring after the fourth trip up and back down that hundred-foot driveway. Now, there was a place to turn around by the garage. So I thought, *why not?* I pulled into this turn-around and started to back up and turn the wheel. Now there was no such thing as power steering in those days, and a 1939 Plymouth was heavy.

So I grunted and pulled on that wheel and started backing up, all at the same time. I felt a little bump but kept on turning and backing. The bumper had caught a short post that I forgot about. The bumper pulled that post into the fender, and mashed a place a foot deep in it, about the

at one end. By the standards of most gyms in the state, it was a "cracker box." But having never played anything but alley ball, I was in heaven in that gym.

If you were male and not crippled, you were expected to play basketball. Now most of the seventh and eighth grade boys had played together since first grade. They all played really well together. They anticipated each other's moves.

Something else too. The gym leaked when it rained, and it had several loose boards. With these obstacles, we could beat just about any other school on our home court. We knew where the puddles and the loose boards were, so we knew when to dribble and when to pass. I had never played organized basketball with a real coach and real fans and real cheerleaders. It was great! But it took me a while to follow the coach's instructions. He actually taught us plays and defense. He taught us to fast break, block out, and all that stuff. I learned the difference between playing man-to-man and a zone defense.

I had never played with my teammates much, so when I got in that first game, I really messed up. I was way too slow to fast break. When I got an open shot, I passed off and would not take the shot. The second and third games were much better after some practices.

Coach Richards learned that I was one of those slow, deliberate players. One night we were playing Union Township School, and they were fast-breaking us to death.

Our guys were supposed to slow down the game, but our guards just kept the game at a super-fast pace. Coach looked down the bench and said, "William, get in the game and slow it down." I became a hero that night.

I walked the ball down the court every time I got my hands on it, set the play, and slowly brought the score to within three points. We called time out with a minute to play. We had possession of the ball. Coach Richards said, "Okay, William, you did a good job. But I need a shooter in the game."

He looked down the bench and nodded to Sam "the man" Ramsey, the best shooter on the team. "Get in the game, Sambo," he said, as he grabbed my jersey and sat me down. It was bittersweet for me. I could not win the game, but then I could not lose it either. The ball inbounded to Bobby Blue, he passed to Sam, and Sam let it fly from fifteen feet. Swish . . . nothing but net.

As the other team inbounded the ball, Johnny Jackson grabbed it for our team and passed back to Sam, who let it fly again. It hit the front of the rim, bounced high in the air, hit the back of the rim, rolled around, and finally dropped in the basket. Five seconds later the horn went off. We won by one point!

I guess that is what teamwork is all about. There were ten players on the team. We all shared in the victory that night. *Lesson learned.* A time to play and a time to sit.

Our school also had a track team. In the spring of the year, we had track and field meets. Remember: I was slow. What events could I compete in? Coach tried me in different events and discovered I was a distance runner.

I could not run fast, but I could run for a long time. So I ran one leg of a relay race, and I ran the four-hundred-forty-yard race. We won a lot of firsts and seconds in the relay race, and I usually ran no worse than second in the four-forty race.

Coach also discovered I was a very good high jumper. I could lope up to the high jump bar, leap, unfold myself, and go over the bar fairly well. He was impressed. On the last track meet of the spring, there were five schools competing. All the races had been run; only the high jump and the pole vault were left. Each team got three tries in the high jump. The best jump counted.

I had just completed my first jump and was in second place. I knew I could jump higher than I did on the first jump. I walked to the bar and eyeballed it. I retraced my steps, took some deep breaths, concentrated, let out my breath halfway, and began my run to the crossbar. Up, up, up and almost over, when my foot caught the crossbar and down we both came.

I threw my arm behind me to break the fall, and fell with my full weight on my arm. I heard a sickening crack that could be heard several feet away, but I did not feel much pain. As I got up, they were putting the bar back up and getting ready for the next jumper. I held up my arm. The hand and wrist hung at a strange angle. Very matter-of-factly, I said, "I broke my arm." No one said anything. So I said it again. Actually, I think I said it three times. One of the judges finally saw my arm and shouted, "Oh my God, he did break his arm!"

There was a man there who had a brand new 1953 Chevrolet. He came up and said, "I'll take him to the hospital." Coach Richards and Miss Holly, who was a teacher, were there, and all three of us got in the back seat of that beautiful two-tone blue Chevy, and we took off for the hospital. It was the fastest ride I had ever taken. He had headers on that thing, and I can still hear the roar of the exhausts and the purring of the engine. It sure did not sound like our old junkers.

I still had no pain, just a throb. That was soon to change. At the hospital, old Doc Coons came in and took a look at my arm. He said, "Hum, broke all right."

Smart man, I thought.

He asked, "Are your parents—", just as they walked in the door. Momma's face was white as a sheet. Daddy had his poker face on. I could never tell if he was mad, sad, or what.

Doc Coons said, "I am going to see what I can do with

this arm." He called a nurse in who was . . . how shall I put this? Fat. Yes, that's the word. She got hold of my elbow, and Doc got hold of my fingers and hand. You could hear the bone crunching. Then there was excruciating pain!

"I better x-ray it," he said, almost to himself. Later, after looking at the x-rays, he said, "I can set it to look pretty, or I can set it so he can use it, but it won't look so nice."

I spoke up and said, "Doc, I need to use my hand and arm!" Daddy nodded his head, and then the fun began.

Nurse "fat butt" on one end, Doc Coons on the other. Crunch, crack, snap, pop. It sounded a lot like Rice Krispies. It hurt like the dickens. I was proud of myself—I didn't say any of the golfing words I had learned. Momma would have washed out my mouth with soap right there in front of God and everybody.

When Doc Coons finished with me that evening, my left arm was bent at a ninety-degree angle at the elbow. It was a real "L-bow" and would be this way for the next three months, all through the hot Indiana summer.

No swimming or baseball, not much of anything. I had always been right-handed. Now I was really right-handed. The only good thing that came out of the injury was that I had an excuse for not washing the dishes and a lot of other chores.

And let me tell you, I "milked" this condition as long as I could.

CHAPTER 13

THE TRIP TO ST. LOUIS

I was beginning to notice the girls more and more. With my arm in a cast and a sling, some of the girls gave me a lot of attention. That was one of the perks of a broken arm.

I was friends with a boy my age whose dad owned a poultry house. They bought and sold eggs and chicken. Old Charlie felt sorry for me that summer. He was going to take a trip to St. Louis to make a contract to buy and sell eggs. His wife and son, Dale, were going with him, and Dale wanted me to go too. So everyone felt sorry for me and I got to go along. It was a great trip. I had never been west of the Indiana state line before. We made the trip in his new two-tone green Plymouth. There was no air conditioning in cars in those days, but we were used to riding with the windows rolled down.

After Charlie conducted his business, we went to see the St. Louis Cardinals play. "Stan the man" Musial was playing and hit a home run. I ate popcorn, cotton candy, peanuts, and drank a big Coke. Wow, it was great! We stayed that night in a motel. The next day we went on a riverboat ride. It was propelled by a paddle wheel. Inside was a big dance floor and a band playing for the people to dance. I pretended I was a famous riverboat gambler back in the 1800s. My imagination ran wild. What a great time!

A girl looking to be about my age came up and stood at the rail, staring down at the dancers. She was dressed in a pretty, frilly, pink dress, complete with crinoline. She was tan and had dark brown eyes. Her long blond hair was done up in a ponytail. She said her name was Sara Jane. Then she asked me how I hurt my arm. I explained how I had almost won first place in a high jump contest. She laid her hand on my shoulder and asked, "Does it hurt much?"

I pretended to wince and said, "Oh yes, at times it sure does." I laid it on pretty thick. Sarah gave me such a sympathetic look, took me by the hand, and led me down to the dance floor. We sat at a table, drank a Coke, watched the dancers, and listened to the band. Then much too soon, the steam whistle sounded and our river ride was over. I never saw Sara Jane again. But I sometimes wonder if she ever thinks, as I do, of that riverboat ride on the Mississippi?

Late that afternoon, we headed back to Indiana. We drove all night and arrived home about six in the morning. Just one more experience, one more memory tucked away in my mind. As Bob Hope always sang when he signed off with on his radio program, "Thanks for the memories." I, too, am thankful for the memories.

CHAPTER 14

ANOTHER MOVE AND ANOTHER SCHOOL

Arriving home one afternoon, I found Daddy lying on the couch sick. "Daddy, what's wrong?"

He just said," I don't know, but I am sick and have pain in my chest."

That evening at Doctor Coons' office, we found out his heart was turning flip-flops in his chest. He never was able to drive the state highway truck again. And so we were back to one paycheck.

We fell behind in the rent and had to move to a smaller house for less rent. This worked out for us in that the smaller house was easier to heat. It was just before school started, and I had to change schools anyway. Washington Township School only went to the eighth grade. We moved about fifteen miles away with the help of uncles, aunts, and cousins. It was a tenant house on a farm that actually had no work hands. There was a government outhouse much better than the one at the other house. We also had running water and a shower in the house. The school was a small county school at a crossroads called Dover.

We rented the house from Mr. Hendricks. He was an old man who had an adopted son. The son, Gordy, dairy-farmed down the road from us. Now Gordy really didn't want to dairy farm. He wanted to be an undertaker.

But Mr. Hendricks had bought Gordy a farm and had set him up in the dairy business to keep him from being drafted. The Korean War had just ended, you see. Gordy was a nice enough young man. He and I kind of hit it off.

Now, I loved farming. I especially loved working with his twenty-six cows. He was set up perfectly so he didn't have to work hard at it.

The cows were milked in what was called a milking parlor. The cows walked in two at a time, and you shut the door behind them, cranked some feed down from a bin overhead, and put the vacuum cups on the cows. The milk ran through plastic tubes directly into the milk can, which was in a cooler behind me. I didn't even have to bend over. The cows were up on a platform about three feet high. Only thing was, if there was a kicker among them, she could kick you in the head. I had some near misses. But the problem with milking is that you have to be there twice a day.

Gordy didn't like to get up early, so I took the early shift, which was five o'clock a.m. I could milk, clean up, and just make the school bus at seven thirty. If I didn't have time to clean up, Gordy was up by seven thirty and he finished up. I worked pretty hard for a sixteen-year-old. I got a few dollars a week, which I turned over to Momma. She needed gas money to get to work.

We were just keeping our heads above water when more hardships came our way. Momma almost had a nervous breakdown. She had had a lot of pressure on her for many years. It finally seemed to catch up to her.

Now, I was going to school, playing basketball, and milking once a day. But a boy needs a break too. Gordy was a stock car fan. Not the NASCAR type. He had a 1941 Ford coupe with a souped-up 1949 Flathead V-8 Mercury engine in it.

Every Saturday night, he went to what was called an "outlaw" racing track up close to Crawfordsville. Since it was an outlaw track, just about anything was allowed. Gordy let me warm the car up a time or two before the race started. What joy for a sixteen-year-old boy, to race around that quarter-mile dirt track in a souped-up Mercury. Now, that was living. My parents never found out about my racing adventure.

Other than cars, my other love was high school basketball. I was never an outstanding player, but I always made the team. Our coach, Herman Smith, was a former Marine drill instructor. He was tough as nails. One day the older boys on the team said they could whip Mr. Smith.

He just laughed at them. They jumped him and tried to pin him to the floor. In a couple of minutes, Mr. Smith had four of them in a pile on the floor, begging for mercy. Funniest thing I ever saw. You see, Mr. Smith stood only about five feet six inches and weighed maybe one hundred fifty pounds. Those smart-alecky farm boys didn't know what hit them.

We were able to stay in the house near Dover for two school years. But we knew we needed to move closer to town. Momma had given up her job at the drugstore due to her health. To get financial aid for families in that day, you had to go to the Township Trustee and practically beg. There were no food stamps then. They didn't give you money. They gave you a voucher for food or fuel from a local store.

It was humiliating because every month, Daddy or Momma would have to go beg for help. If it had been up to me, I would have starved. I often went all day without eating. I could not afford the thirty-five cents for the school lunch.

Some of the local farmers around there learned that I was not going to get an athletic sweater because of the cost. But when it came time to order, some kind person had ordered and paid for mine. I never learned who it was. It was a beige sweater with a dark brown "D" on the front. Now I had two athletic sweaters. The other one I earned was red with a big "W" on it from Washington Township

School. The person who paid for my sweater had no idea what it did for my ego. This was a great lesson for me. If you can assist a young person when he or she is down, you must do it. I believe I became a better person from that one act of kindness.

It was while I was at Dover School that I also discovered girls. My sister had left a bad taste in my mouth about girls. Mary Anne had recently married and moved from home. But these country girls were different. They were more like boys, only in dresses. They could drive tractors and farm trucks like a man. Some of them went rabbit hunting with their dads. I suspected one or two of them took a chew now and then.

I remember Sarah Walker, the beautiful daughter of the man who drove my school bus. She had blond hair and blue eyes. I always grabbed the seat beside her and put my arm up over the back of the seat. She played hard to get and pretty much ignored me. Her dad never did say anything to me, but he kept a sharp eye on me in the mirror.

Then there were the two Galloway girls. I would smile, wink, and flirt with them, until I found out their dad was a state trooper. I didn't want to mess with the daughters of a man who could give me a ticket.

The prettiest and most popular girls came in threes.

There were three of the McGowan sisters: Gerri, Janet, and Jeanie. The closest I got to a date was a Sunday School party at their house one time. The old sourpuss of a preacher was there. He didn't seem to trust us kids. He kept the boys separated from the girls. I didn't like his preaching much anyway.

Since the only car I had to drive was our old beat-up Chevy that constantly had flat tires, I never asked any of the above-mentioned girls for a date. Actually, I couldn't afford a date anyway.

However, this reminds me of one of my Saturday trips to the village of Thorntown. As I previously said, Daddy never believed in spending money on new tires. He always said it was a waste of money. We kept several spare tires mounted on wheels in the trunk, with one behind the driver's seat as well.

I had to run an errand for Momma that day. Before I got to Thorntown, I had two flat tires about five miles apart. I put on the best ones I could find in the trunk. I had gotten pretty good at using the bumper jack and the lug wrench. I drove the rest of the way to the village with the tires thumping from the boots in them. One particular tire was bumping pretty good, but I ignored it, hoping it would not go flat before I got back home.

I pulled up to a stop sign on a side street in town. I sat there gunning the engine, listening to the rumble of the exhaust. A little boy who looked to be no more than five years old was playing on the sidewalk. He had on a cowboy hat that was two sizes too large for his head. He also had a six-shooter in his hand, which he pointed at me and fired. It was a cap pistol, and he emptied that thing at me. Pop. Pop. Pop. Pop.

I squinted up, aimed my finger at him, and pretended to shoot him back. So help me, if I'm lying, I'm dying. No sooner had I pointed my finger at him, the back tire closest to the little boy blew out—seriously! Bang! Well, sir, that little guy went running in the house screaming for his mommy.

I really didn't want to change another tire, but the expression on that little cowboy's face was worth it. His Momma came out carrying him, and he was still stifling a sob. I gave her a detailed description of what had happened. Fortunately, she saw more humor in it than her little cowboy did. I kept telling the little guy I was sorry, but he would have none of it.

CHAPTER 15

ANOTHER MOVE

Life in the country was good for me but not all that good for my folks. The first time I saw that little house, I said to myself, "You have got to be kidding me." At one time, it must have been a garage or something. It only had two rooms—a small kitchen and a small bathroom. I had to sleep on a cot in the corner of my parents' bedroom. By this time, Daddy had recovered somewhat and took a job doing light janitor work in a glove factory.

Shortly after our move back to town, Momma also began to get her nerves back together. A friend of ours from the Dover area was able to help Momma get a job as a claims clerk in an insurance company. It was a good job for her. So we were back to a two-paycheck family again.

Uncle Don moved us again in his old farm truck. We got the double bed, my cot, couch, chair, and kitchen table in the house. We all sat down on the couch and in the chair. Don looked over at us and said, "You can't cuss a cat in this house, it's so small." We all laughed a nervous laugh at his remark. It was true, but it was all we could afford. I vowed we would do better sometime.

You see, my folks had never owned a house or even a decent car. I made a vow that I would do better than my folks had done. At age sixteen, I was ashamed of my folks, our little house, our junk car, and our "used-up" tires.

Now I am ashamed that I felt that way.

Booneville High School was the largest school I had ever attended. I recognized some of the kids from my early years at Harney Elementary. But I had no really close friends. I still had a close friend at Dover. For some reason, John Rains had chosen me as a friend. He was from a well-to-do family. His dad owned a grocery store at Dover.

John was a worker. He trapped for pelts in the winter and ran a paper route year-round. He knew how to handle money. That was something I had never had to do. How can you handle something you can't get your hands on?

Well, John and I ran around some. He came to Booneville every chance he got. John had saved his money and one day he drove up in the most beautiful car I had ever seen. A brand-new, dark green Pontiac. He had paid cash for it from the money he had saved through the years.

I learned something that year. Girls like new cars. John and I became quite popular. But we never got serious about any one girl. It was about this time I realized I needed to have an after-school job if I was going to ever own that house and new car I vowed I would have.

Somehow, I found out about a job setting pins at a local bowling alley. It was from right after school until about midnight, three nights a week, and on Saturday. Now, back then there were few restrictions on how long a teenager could work. I took advantage of this opportunity and worked as much as I could.

People operated bowling alleys then. The bowler would roll his ball and when it knocked down the pins, I would pick up the ball, roll it back up the alley, put the pins that had been knocked down back on the pin rack, and pull a cord to reset the pins. Each person took care of two alleys. This all happened at a quick pace and you really had to hustle.

Bowling balls are not light. Pins are not light, and they are not padded. Sometimes I would get struck by a pin. I went home with bruises many a night.

The bowling alley had league nights, which were really good because they tipped well. I only made fifty cents per hour, but the tips were good. I sometimes took home ten or fifteen dollars a night.

This was the most money I had ever had in my possession at the end of the week. I learned to manage money. Some people called me tight, or miser, or skinflint. I didn't care. However, there was still a problem. My parents were still strapped financially, and I had to help them with bills for a while.

Between trying to keep my grades up and working so late, there was no time for sports. I doubt I could have made the team anyway. For the first time in my youth, I did not play baseball or basketball. But I learned to work and save money.

Strange as it may sound to this modern generation, as I look back on my life, I often thank the Lord that I was not born rich and privileged. Because, you see, I would have never learned to work or to save money or be able to purchase a home. I would have never become excited about a new car or a color television if all these things had just been handed to me.

I have learned many lessons through the years. Wars eventually come to an end. Dogs grow old and die. Friends move away. Calves were not meant to ride. Don't cuss where adults can hear you. Whisky is not as good as it looks in the movies. A person does not have to be the star player to enjoy the victory. Pies do not always land right side up. Finally and perhaps the greatest lesson is that neither good times nor bad times are permanent.

These were but a few of the lessons Peanut, Mary Ann, my cousins, and I learned back then.

How shall I sum up these times about which I have written? The best description I have for these times are bound up in four key words: *innocent, simple,* sometimes *difficult*, and yet when combined, they were the *best* of times.

TIME MARCHES ON

In his seventy-fifth year, as he was being rolled into the operating room at the Methodist Hospital in Indianapolis, the old man thought of a boy he once knew. Why? He had no idea, except he had not fulfilled his vow to keep in touch. If he failed to awaken, he hoped God would not hold this broken vow against him.

Where was William? Was he still alive? Did he have grandchildren? Did he ever think of the grand old times they had together? In his mind, Ronnie Neal could still picture William sitting on his special limb in that special cherry tree. He remembered the time William's mother threatened to climb that tree if he didn't come down and take the licking he deserved. He smiled to himself as he drifted off into that wonderful sleep induced by a masked man staring down at him.

At about the same time, two states away in Tennessee, an old man by the name of William Henry sat in a boat on Watts Bar Lake, drowning worms. The sun was on his face, and he was as content as he had been in years. For some reason at that moment, he thought of a boy he had once known so well. Peanut was his name. Actually, it was Ronnie, but he went by Peanut. Now what was it that caused him to think of a boy he had not seen in almost seventy years?

He would have loved to share that moment at the lake with that boy Peanut and old Buck, William's faithful canine. William had made many friends over the years but none as close as Peanut. He had also had many dogs in his life but none as loyal as Buck.

Of all his friends and close relatives, none were still living. His parents, his sister, his aunts and uncles had all died. He had even outlived his children. He only had one living granddaughter.

He wished he had kept in touch with Peanut, but there must be hundreds of men named Ronnie Neal. It would take a miracle to find him. That's what he needed, a miracle. William silently prayed, "Lord, send me a miracle."

As the old man awoke from his bypass surgery, a pretty nurse came in the room to check his vitals. The name tag on her uniform read, Nancy Henry, RN. The next day, that pretty nurse came in again and said, "Mr. Neal, are you feeling better today?"

He said he was but he had a question. "I once knew some people named Henry years ago. Would you be related to them by any chance?"

"I don't know," she said. "My daddy's name is Robert. He was named after my great-grandfather."

Mr. Neal asked, "And what was your grandfather's name?"

"His name is William. He's retired and lives in Tennessee."

The old man's eyes opened wide, and he said, "Did you say his name is William? Did he ever live over in Booneville?"

The young nurse replied, "Why, yes, as a matter of fact he did, for many years."

Tears began to form at the corner of the old man's eyes and rolled down his cheek. The young nurse said, "Sir, are you all right? Can I get you something? Are you in pain?"

The old man said, "No. I am just fine. Tell me, did you have a great aunt by the name of Mary Anne?"

She looked somewhat surprised and said, "Yes, Aunt Mary Anne has been dead about twenty years now."

The old man's face screwed up; he was weeping. He could hardly say anything for a moment, but he held that nurse's hand tightly as he swallowed hard and finally said, "Your granddaddy was my best friend in all the world when I was just a boy. I would give anything to see him or even talk to him on the phone one more time."

After the shift changed that evening, Nancy Henry came back into the room. She had her cell phone in her hand. She said, "Mr. Neal, would you like to talk to my granddaddy? I can dial him right now."

The old man had a lump in his throat as he said, "Oh, sweet lady, how I would love to talk to William." The number was dialed and after a short conversation, the nurse handed the phone to the old man.

This conversation was just too emotional, too precious, and too sacred to eavesdrop on, so Nancy left the room. The call went on for about half an hour. Phone numbers and addresses were exchanged. It was the miracle William told him he'd prayed for while sitting in his boat on Watts Bar Lake.

Perhaps Ronnie would see his childhood best friend again. They would talk about the war they had helped to win with their ridiculous-looking homemade weapons. They would speak of their scrap drives and snowball fights. They would remember the adventures planned while sitting in the most wonderful, yellow cherry tree. They would laugh at how Mrs. Patterson would smack their hands with a ruler for throwing paper wads.

Oh, what a wonderful miracle God had given these two little boys, now grown old. They had kept their vow after all, and now they could have peace at last.

In a couple of months, the old man recovered from his bypass surgery and was feeling better than he had felt in years. Either he or William would phone each other at least once a week, and they would talk for half an hour or so at a time.

One day several months later, William told Peanut, "This is too costly. Why don't you come down and visit me on the lake?" This was discussed with Nancy and some of the other family members. On his seventy-seventh birthday, the family presented Peanut with an airline ticket to Knoxville, Tennessee, and a card explaining that William Henry would meet him at the airport.

Two days later, Peanut was sitting in William's bass boat on Watts Bar Lake. Just two old men sitting in a boat pretending to be fishing.

They talked and laughed about the ghosts in William's "haunted house." William told again how that fox squirrel had chased him out of his room. Peanut reminded William about their adventures at the old Harney School. Catching each other up on what had taken place in their lives took about three days. They talked of their children and grandchildren. They spoke about their failures, successes, and the disappointments in their lives.

They told each other about their employment before they retired. Peanut had gone into business for himself when he was thirty-five years old. He had worked with a man who was a plumbing and electrical contractor. Peanut had bought out the contractor's business when he retired. And so for almost forty years, he had run a very successful business. He had only recently sold it to a young man who had worked for him the last ten years.

William had become a preacher, of all things. Peanut had a good laugh over this. He said he could not imagine William as a minister. William said not only had he been a minister, but he still filled in occasionally for preachers who were taking sabbaticals. He said, "Peanut, I think I will just baptize you while I have you out on the lake." They had another big laugh about that. They talked for hours about all of those things—most of all, reminiscing about their boyhood adventures in a small town during World War II.

William asked Peanut about his siblings, Jimmy and Libby. Jimmy died in 2001, and Libby was in a nursing home suffering from dementia. All these two old men had were each other and the most wonderful memories a person could have of an innocent time in childhood. William looked over at Peanut and softly said, "God is so good."

Peanut whispered, "Amen."

The visit lasted two weeks. Both William and Peanut had outlived their wives. Actually, Peanut had outlived two.

For two weeks, the two elderly men had a grand old time. They fished on the lake, rocked in the sun on the porch, cooked their own meals, and occasionally ate out. Sometimes they went to the Cracker Barrel or a steakhouse. Sometimes they had breakfast at Hardees with a table full of other old men. All the while, a table full of old ladies eyeballed the old men and whispered.

The day came for them to bid each other farewell. They said goodbye at the Knoxville airport. While sitting in the car at the airport, William took Peanut's hand, bowed his head, and prayed. He asked God to bless both of them until they saw each other again.

William watched that silver bird climb until it became just a dark speck against the blue sky. He was pretty sure Peanut was looking down at him, with a tear streaming down his cheek.

The two men continued to speak by phone every few weeks. They recounted those innocent days of their boyhood. They probably repeated the same stories over again, but they laughed every time. These conversations seemed to revitalize both of them.

Then a few months later, Peanut received word that William had left this world. He had a sudden stroke, and it took him instantly. William's body was being flown back to Booneville for the funeral.

Peanut was present at the graveside of William Henry that cool spring day in April. The preacher made a few generic remarks, but one could tell he knew nothing about William. Finally, the preacher asked if there were any others who wanted to say something.

Nancy Henry made a few tearful remarks about her grandfather. After a few moments of silence, another voice said, "I want to say something please."

The old man with the oddly-shaped head stood on unsteady legs and softly said, "This man was the best friend I ever had as a child. I thought for many years I would never see him again, but by the grace of God and a miracle, we found each other." He then placed his hand on the casket and whispered, "So long, buddy. I will be along in a little while. But until then, could you save a limb in that old cherry tree for me?"

ABOUT THE AUTHOR

Phil Emmert began his second career when he left a secure job with the Dow Chemical Company in Indiana, where he was a research assistant. At age thirty-three, he sold his little farm near Lebanon, Indiana, and enrolled in Johnson Bible College near Knoxville, Tennessee. Upon his graduation, he went into the full-time ministry, preaching in several different Christian Churches and Churches of Christ.

Phil has worn many hats in his seventy-eight years. He has been an animal technician, part time farmer, research assistant, school bus driver, substitute school teacher, children's social worker, and a Juvenile Crime Prevention counselor in a county school system. All the while he was ministering to small churches in Tennessee and North Carolina. Phil still drives over one hundred miles round trip, twice a week, to preach and teach in a small country church.

From all these experiences with people and especially with children, Phil became aware that young people are ignorant of American history. Therefore at the age of seventy-seven, he began his third career by completing his first book in this two-book series, When War Was Heck. He is now working on his third book, which he describes as a "Christian Romance."

Phil is the father of four adult children of which he says, *"They are my greatest accomplishments."* He has eleven grandchildren. He also has three adult stepchildren.

Phil is optimistic that all who read *When War Was Heck* and *The Afterglow of War: Lessons Learned* will find themselves emotionally involved with William, Peanut, Mary Ann, and Buck the Border Collie. The older generation who read these stories will find themselves identifying with the characters. Phil hopes love of country will be awakened in young people as they read these stories. Above all, he hopes these accounts give everyone a greater appreciation for those who have preceded our present generation.